No One Left to Touch

& Other Stories

Elizabeth Greyrose

Dedicated to all my friends who met me where I was, a little lost and confused about who and where I wanted to be. Thanks for the dances, the pub visits, night swimming, and welcoming me into your homes.

Sorry all I can offer in return is a book dedication and the occasional vampire movie marathon.

Contents

Preface

No *One Left to Touch and Other Stories* came about in a strange way. I had not originally planned on creating something like this with the short stories that I wrote during 2024–2026. However, I saw many shared themes. Two themes were the phases of a life and the phases of womanhood: Maiden, Mother, Crone, Eternity, and Death. Yet, I did not want a story about motherhood or girlhood. I have written these themes so many times in my previous work under my own name, especially in Vampires of the Paper Flower Consortium. Two stories in the anthology, "Monday Night Hunger" and "Last Gasp of Roseton" were originally in a general market, but there was always more to the story, and I expanded both for this anthology.

I do not believe sex is a sin. I believe one of the fundamental gifts of humanity is that we are able to enjoy intercourse outside of estrus. Yet, I can be shy about speaking about such things. Or even speaking about myself. In my mid-40s, suddenly, I lost my voice. However, I never lost my love for writing. Or for horror.

Erotic horror is a genre older than we like to think. Vampire stories with the monster as an erotic figure have been popular since at least the 18th century, with works like "The Bride of Corinth" by Goethe (1797), *Carmilla* by Joseph Sheridan Le Fanu, and *The Vampyre* by John Polidori (1819) and of course the ever popular *Dracula* by Bram Stoker (1897). However, even earlier, we have stories of succubi, sirens, and other creatures who prey on young men — either in their dreams or in the wild — described in ancient myths worldwide. Trolls, giants, goblins, and even dragons stealing young women as wives appear in fairy tales. I cannot pretend that I am doing something new. However, I hope people enjoy reading these stories and I am connecting with them through the written word.

My other truth, and yours too, dear reader, is that life is beautiful and precious. There is so much joy and there are so many times you just want to scream. It's shorter than we pretend. Before you know it, it's half over. Then two-thirds over. I don't know what fraction fits in my case. None of us know how long we have. However, I knew I wanted to learn to dance. At 46, I used research as an excuse to take my first waltz lesson — though I had wanted to do it since I was 30. Fear stopped me then. So did life, and the career I told myself had to come first. Then I began to dance. I learned the rotary waltz, then lindy, then cross-step waltz, then contra and other folk dances. I danced four or five times a week. Hell, maybe I'll die tomorrow — but I learned to dance.

I'm not exaggerating. My life is at least half over. My fourth decade of life, and its companion perimenopause, hit me hard. I almost quit writing. I told myself no one wanted to read what I wrote anymore — that I was too old, completely out of touch. My oldest clothes are vintage; some of my furniture is older than some of my friends. That's where "Second Hand Dress" and "Olivia's Mirror" came from. I have outlived friends who were younger than me. Two took their own lives. One had a fucking heart attack before the age of fifty — in this century. What the actual fuck? My best friend is alive, thank the universe, but a pulmonary embolism nearly killed her. She is three years younger than me.

However, life is miraculous when we slow down enough to see it. I found a group of newer friends, some younger than me and just as many older. I'm right in the middle, because I'm middle-aged! I began going to after-parties. I began sitting at kitchen tables again, having conversations. I wanted to explore life in a way I hadn't before. I even began organizing my own waltz after seeing a gap in the community.

Real friends. People I can rely upon. When a friend died, they pressed together in a group hug — platonic and very necessary. In that moment, my old hurts rose up, and I told them I was glad I hadn't cried publicly. They said they wouldn't have cared if I needed to. My voice broke. What they, and I, didn't realize was that it was my heart breaking open. Becoming. Two weeks later, I would cry publicly. I would apologize for it as my friend tried to calm me or let me cry. No one left me. All he said was, he didn't think I should have to apologize for big feelings.

My writing was becoming rawer and more erotic, and yet I hesitated to claim that label. Sex, monsters, and death have been intertwined since ancient times, and my erotic voice grew stronger as those themes became more interesting to me. People say women don't want sex during menopause — I wanted it, even when my body wasn't cooperating. That inspired "Ghost on the Internet."

I love my husband with such passion that a cross word left me weepy. Perimenopause turns small moments into crises — there were many misunderstandings. I began having panic attacks. I had one on the dance floor. That was why I wrote "Monday Night Hunger." I began fearing my husband's death. I began thinking about my own, and I did not fear it for myself as much as I feared for my parents, my siblings, my friends. That became "The Last Gasp of Roseton" and "No One Left to Touch."

I don't know how long any of us have, but I am choosing to live my life the best I can. I joined a few more creative groups. One meets in a bookshop where I draw with other visual artists. My second writing group meets in someone's home — and admittedly, sometimes I slip off to the couch to write sex scenes, because it is genuinely strange to do that while people work and eat popcorn or apples nearby.

But that's life, and life is worth celebrating. And honestly, it was the only way this book would have been finished before Norwescon, 2026!

Dear reader, I hope you enjoy this anthology.

Elizabeth

Endless Love

Contained in a Willow

"Have you seen my Thaddaeus?" I call.

The young couple does not acknowledge my cry. Not yet. They are too in love with each other as they caress under my weeping branches. I shake the whiplike tertiary branches of the willow. Leaves fall. So do a few spiders, caterpillars, and gnats. The birds nesting in my willow's crown take flight. Their sorrowful chirps, twanging and resounding, tinkling and squabbling, full of lust and territorial anger as I stretch withing my wooden tomb careful to not push past its strength. I want this generations and more to find their home within my branches. Though ultimately unneeded, the presence of small lives is lovely to me. I want them.

The two young people jump to their feet and wipe the arthropods away from their clothing and shake out their hair. They laugh. They are in love.

I call: "I seek my Thaddeus; will you help me? He was once a legionnaire, now bone only exists, if at all."

They look up; they heard me. One points upward. I reach for them. With his hand gripping the girl's wrist, the lad backs away. She follows. They do not move fast enough to escape my tendrils of leaves.

"I hear his cry; my heart aches to find him," I say.

My wooden fingers from my thicker branches slice into their fleshy bits, only slowed temporarily by their bones. Their bodies, human bodies, are so fragile, as mine once was. "Fear not I am not vengeful. I exist in this tree to find my love, Thaddeus. Have you seen him?" I ask.

Instead of answering, they scream in nonsensical terror and pain as once living humans often do. Blood leaks from their mouths, from their wide, weeping eyes. Their blood slips to the ground, soaking my roots, softening the dirt. Their feces enriches the soil around my rootbase. And I tell my story as my first order branches pummel their bodies until the bones are a calcium-rich dust which I will feed upon. I look for the spirits of those who I have killed, but they do not seem to be here. Perhaps, their love was not as wondrous as my own. Still I sing my song and tell their decaying corpses how I became trapped in a willow.

Before I was a ghost, locked within the rings of a tree, I was a girl with black braids, skin browned by the sun, who danced with my flute, and had no idea why the men were fighting. All I knew was my great love for Thaddaeus.

Thaddaeus had his toga virilis ceremony. He wore his first beard with pride. I left my lunula with my childhood dresses and toys and put on my mother's oldest dress. I quietly traveled as his concubine with his legion. Though not a thousand prayers to Juno could break Roman law and allow us to marry, I kept his tent and managed our small household as a Roman woman should. Most of Thaddius's men referred to me as his wife.

Strong and virile, I thought Thaddius might live forever. I thought he would fight in a thousand battles. He survived few. The battle was closing in that day. Our camp would be overrun, but we did not live to see that. In some ways, my death means I was fortunate. My body was his alone. My love for him alone. An arrow hit his leg, and the blood gushed, wetting the battlefield. He fell to his knees. From our tent, I heard him and other men screaming.

I raced to him, trying to block the onslaught of another volley of arrows with a fallen shield. The blood kept spilling. His veins brutally severed. The gray, uncaring sun burned down on us, pitiless. Another volley of arrows darkened the sky. My body was pierced by a dozen arrows after I fell. The pain in my heart was screaming, perhaps I was screaming, trying to save him. My legs were on fire. My shoulders, my neck. And my blood would not stop flowing into his.

I looked at his brown eyes for the last time, and he gazed into mine. Clasping my face and drawing me near so that when the ferryman came, he whispered, "We will travel the River Styx together?" In those last bloody moments, before I bled out, I wondered if did Thaddaeus feared we would be parted? And for the first time, I felt the fear of death. We were of unequal status. He fought in battles, but I was simply a woman in love, a plebian concubine. I would receive no honor. No one would write songs about me. Most did not know my name. Tradition claimed I would be bound to the Plain of Asphodel while he would move on to Elysium.

Thaddeus's friends lifted him on their shoulders. Thaddeus was wrapped in the finest linen. His eulogies told by his two other soldiers proudly spoke of the successes and great deeds of Thadeaus's father and his grandfather. His friends believed he would be destined for the Elysium Fields. Letters were sent, and our commander spoke of his great deeds before his death. My body was brutalized by the battle and trampled in the mud. However, because his men, all men, believed those who died "before their natural term" or without proper funeral rites were thought to wander the earth and haunt the living as vengeful, vagrant ghosts, they picked up my crushed body and dumped it into Thaddeus's grave.

Together, our spirits learned there is no glory in war unless you are a king or a senator. Though Thaddeous was of a patrician family, he did not have a documentarian in his tent.

The was no need, he had been young. He should have seen many battles. We both rotted, fed on by worms. Our milky eyes and juicy tongues went first. We both rotted and our souls broke free from our mortal coil. Perhaps the ferryman could not find us, hidden from view. We mingled our soul in the grave. Time had no meaning. Life had no meaning. We were one, in a way that we could never be in life.

And I was happy for we died in the truest young love. Forever. Immortal.

Until a fluffy willow seed fly in the breeze and landed between us, germinating.

One day, something hard grew up between us, intertwining me, tangling my bones as it pressed upward toward the sun. My beloved began to scream my name as he was pushed the other way. I screamed his. I was pressed towards the sky digitus by digitus. I spiral the tree roots and feel the tree growing. I moved up the gray and smooth trunk, which eventually cracked and became brown with age. I sang to my love, I shook the branches, and spread the seeds of love.

I sweep the bone dust and bloodied earth of my victims around my rootbase with my leafy tendrils. And I hear Thaddaeus, but I lost him in the twisting roots. The willow spreads. And the wood shifts and moves as the wind blows its seeds and corns to and fro.

I call my love to the insects with flowers and hairy fruit.

I call to the bees and the beetles. The willow flea weevil deposits her eggs on the bottom of the willow leaves. Her larvae dig through the leaf. The wasps build their own nest in my branches and the wild gossamer texture of spiderwebs crisscross my trees fore the arboreal spiders eat the flea weevil. Camouflaged against the bark, tree frogs declare their intentions with breeding croaks. Snakes drape in my weeping branch and nestle between my roots hoping to catch a bird or a frog.

Fed by blood, bone, and excrement, I push my lateral roots forward, seeking my love, who is lost somewhere in the earth. Buried. Not breathing fore, he has no need; yet suffocating for eternity.

I know he is close, keening for me. Lost underneath my tap roots. He prays to find me, or I find him. I do not keen, but sing a dirge in my victim's blood. Letting him know I am here even if we cannot touch...yet. His keening grows more potent as my taproot grows deeper. Closer to my lost love's soul, buried in the soil for decades, perhaps it is centuries. Time has no meaning or relevance to my memories.

In the summer, when the leaves create dappled shadows, young human lovers take shelter in my leaves and make often in secret make love under the willow trees.

Do they hear the echoes of my love for Thaddeus? I wonder. And because the weather is warm and the sky is bright, soon another young couple appears. I droop my leaves to hide the blood-stained ground. I whisper that I am shelter from prying eyes. Giggling, the young couple enter my cover of leaves.

I whisper, "Have you seen my Thadius?"

They are lost in their love; they do not hear me. They will.

I began Endless Love Contained in a Willow in the Fall 2024 but set it aside, unable to identify what was missing. My original intention was to write about eternal love. Returning to it in 2026, I understood the problem: the story needed to explore how eternal love can drive one to madness. Because my main character dies as a girl, she remains a girl in eternity — her love undying and passionate, yet incapable of fulfillment.

Second Hand Dress, Haunted

Kayla flips through the hangers at one of her preferred second-hand shops. Her 90s playlist sings in her ears as she moves from hanger to hanger. A thought lingers: This is the only place I truly belong. She pauses to pull out a satin blouse and sniffs. The scent of mothballs and mildew wafts up—a complex smell that's difficult to remove from the delicate fabric. She loves 90s music: Nirvana, The Cure, and Smashing Pumpkins.

At twenty-two years old, Kayla feels disillusioned with modern life. The 1990s, in her mind, was the last free decade, where most people were untethered to cell phones and social media. She hates the constant bing of texts and direct messages. Yet, she cannot understand how life had moved without them: not having a phone seemed even more foreign.

A peculiar blue and white pattern catches her attention: an empire-style mini-dress. Outwardly, it is a simple cotton knit, yet its presence feels strange and otherworldly. She can't look away. The tag tells her the garment is storebought. However, the garment's hem and cuffs are extended by a strip of contrasting fabric, sewn by hand with nonuniform but carefully crafted stitches. It's so simple, this dress should not intrigue her so.

Kayla slips her hand into the pocket and feels a crinkle. She pulls out an old photograph: four teenagers—three boys and a girl—stand in front of a modest house. A few years younger than herself. Probably 17 or 18, just as they were starting their adult lives, getting ready for college.

The girl is wearing this dress. The back of the photo lists: Jonathan, Jake, Scott, and Melissa, '94. If the photo's names are in the order of the shot, then she can see each face with clarity and name each one.

Kayla feels a strange connection to Melissa, a familiarity she can't explain. Her expression is young and carefree and she has what they used to call bedroom eyes as she gazes at the boy who presumably was Scott.

There is something else about the photo Kayla cannot place. She studies it, lingering on every detail. The house in the background—she knows it. She rides her bike past it almost every day on her way to work. How strange.

Kayla brings the dress to the counter and shows the clerk the photo. "I'd like the dress, but I found this in the pocket."

"Keep it," the clerk says in a bored voice. "Just an old photo."

At home, Kayla carefully launders the dress in vinegar. She checks the seams, especially the extensions. Once it is dry and ironed, she slips it on. The knit is soft with age, and the dress fits her perfectly as if it were made for her. Yet, seeing her reflection in the dress, she wishes she looked as authentic as Melissa. She presses her hair into the side part common to the era. That helps.

She begins hearing her favorite songs in her head. Only they are different somehow.

A compulsion surges through her. She must deliver the photo back to its home.

"It's the middle of the night," she mumbles to herself.

Kayla means to remove the dress, but cannot bear to take it off just yet—it fits so perfectly. She lies down in it, telling herself she will not fall asleep or she will wake up rumpled.

That night, she dreams of the girl: Melissa. She wears the dress, a pair of Doc Martens, and a matching flannel. Melissa happily says to Kayla, "Look, we are twins."

Melissa reaches out to touch Kayla's hand. Kayla is obliged

to take the ghost's hands as they dance to her music.

Her eyes are milky and hollow. Melissa's body rots, decaying to the beat of the song. The ghostly vision pulls Kayla away from her bed and home, singing songs with an uncanny, haunting voice.

Melissa and Kayla are in the sky, one with the world. One with each other.

Melissa wraps her arms about Kayla in a simple, gracious hug and yet, there is more. Kayla is sure she feels more. Their skin is soft and their lips are yielding to each other.

Kayla knows she was born in the wrong time. She yearns for the 90s.

Melissa laughs brightly and shakes her head.

Then she begins to sing. While Melissa knows all the songs, the lyrics are different from the ones Kayla knows. Kayla wants to argue and tries to show Melissa a modern playlist. "That's not what the singer says," she insists, fumbling for her phone as proof.

Melissa ignores her as she sways to the music. "You experience it your way, I'll experience it mine."

"But you're wrong!"

"Am I? These songs only exist in my heart."

Kayla wakes with a start. Her skin is clammy and cold. The dress is drenched in sweat. Kayla pulls her arm out of the sleeve and begins to wrench it over her head. Though she wishes to remove the dress, she reinserts her arm into the sleeve and smooths the knit over her torso.

Nervous as she is feeling, she is also strangely annoyed.

Opening her music app, Kayla looks up the lyrics. Every word the girl sang felt right, even when they were not the correct lyrics. It was as if she was singing from the musician's very soul—or perhaps Kayla's soul. Melissa knows the songs in a way that Kayla never will. Melissa was there. She lived in the era.

Kayla does not know why she wishes Melissa was wrong, but she does. Though she is coated in sweat and wants to shower and change, it seems wrong to take off the dress. Disrespectful to the memory of Melissa and to the 1990s. "I will return the photo to its home, today!" She decides aloud.

Kayla stands before the neglected house; she feels as if she has walked into an uncanny valley. It looks eerily similar to the one in the photo. Time has left scars in the painted siding, but the exterior remains intact. The front door is cast in the shadows of unkempt shrubbery.

She knocks on the door.

An unshaven man, probably in his 50s, answers. His eyes

widen when he sees her. "Who are you? Where did you get that dress?"

"I'm Kayla," she stammers. "I found the dress at a second-hand shop. There was this photo in the pocket, and I thought it might belong to you. I recognized the house."

She hands him the photo and suppresses the urge to throw her arms around his neck. She doesn't know this man yet he feels more than familiar. *He is family.*

The man nods slowly. "Oh, it must have been with my sister's...things."

"Are you in the photo?" Kayla asks.

His brow furrows. With a slight smile, he says, "Yeah. I'm there. Jonathan. Those were good times." The smile vanishes as quickly as it had appeared. He thrusts the photo back at Kayla. "But it doesn't matter."

Kayla fumbles for words. "What, why?"

"They're all gone."

"Gone?" Kayla asks, though she is sure he means dead.

"I'm the last one left."

"I'm so sorry for your loss."

He shakes his head. "Nothing to be sorry for. Car accident." He gestures toward the photo. "Keep it. I don't want it."

"I could leave it at their resting place," she offers hesitantly.

He huffs. "Do whatever you want with it."

Overwhelmed by his uncaring attitude, she asks, "Where were they laid to rest?"

"Belle View Mortuary," he mutters. "Melissa and Jake are side by side. Scott is one row up. Our parents fought with him about the placement...so stupid now."

"Thank you," Kayla says softly. "I'm truly sorry for your loss."

She steps forward before she can stop herself and throws her arms around him. He stiffens but doesn't pull away.

"I forgive you," she might have said. She isn't sure if the words popped out of her mouth or not. After a moment, she lets go and walks away, the breeze tugging at the dress as if urging her to return to Melissa's brother. She wants to ask if he is married. Where does he work? Does he like it? However, Jonathan certainly would not answer Kayla. She is a stranger.

"Hey, Miss," Jonathan calls. "Young lady."

Kayla turns back for a moment.

"You're too young to dress like that."

Kayla is shocked, but she throws her shoulders back. Is he one of those type of men? "The world isn't like that anymore, old man!" Kayla hisses and turns to go.

"Get rid of it!" Jonathan shouts.

Embarrassed, she climbs on her bike and pedals as fast as she can down the street, the photo still in her pocket. She will deliver the photo, she must deliver the photo!

At the cemetery, she brings three small bouquets and begins searching systematically. Finally, she finds the three graves: Melissa and Jake side by side, Scott one row up. She places the photo on Melissa's stone and lays flowers on all three. A profound loneliness washes over Kayla as she stands in the quiet. She reaches for her phone to turn on her music but hesitates. The songs are now a reminder of something lost, something distant. It was an innocent time but also a time with its own challenges. She feels older somehow, as if she lived those years rather than seeing them through rose-colored glasses. Melissa, Jake, and Scott lost their lives during this time.

As she turns to leave, she sees him. Jonathan stands at the edge of the cemetery, watching her.

The haunted dress grows warm, and Kayla feels a shift, electrifying the air around her—as if something is being peeled from in between the weaves of the fabric itself.

Melissa's ghost is free. The dress no longer moves on its own. Indeed, the dress is hers. Completely hers.

Kayla wants to go, but has nowhere to go. She can go to her classes or to her job, but what of it? She would still be here. The now familiar compulsion whispers, "lie down." She lowers herself onto the soft grave and hears the faint strumming of a distorted electric guitar. Drums. A vocalist cries about her social isolation. That's where the music is. Melissa knows the songs in a way that Kayla never will.

"Don't," Jonathan calls.

She hears his footsteps pound toward her. She doesn't care. She presses her ear to the grave to hear the music better.

"Come to me," a voice whispers. "I'm lonely."

The dress presses against Kayla's body and she feels a sharp tug from below. The music grows louder for a moment, then silence. There is no music in the grave!

Kayla tries to twist free. She tries to lift her head away from the earth, but the dress presses on her torso, her thighs, pressing her deeper.

Grit scratches her bare calves, envelops her hair. She is pulled deeper, her face hits the ground, the pressure on her skin is massive. The smell of rot overwhelms her.

Kayla tries to squirm free from the garment. She twists, gets one arm out and reaches upward toward the sky. She feels rough hands yank her back away from the grave.

Is that Jonathan? Did he come to save me?

Kayla tightens her grip as she tries to assist him in assisting her. Above her, he begins screaming. A furious rage rips through her.

She is sure she said—or possibly Melissa said—"I don't forgive you for killing us."

Or at least Melissa tried to say it, but so much moldering, rotten dirt is in her mouth and nostrils, scratching her eyes.

She tries to scream. Every sound is muffled by earth. As if caught in a tide, Kayla is pulled deeper. Trying to hold her breath, she gropes for freedom. Rot fills her nostrils. She touches something squishy. A piece of rotting, distended flesh bursts under the pressure of her hand. She grips the skeletal bones.

Her lungs feel as if they may burst. She begins to retch. She reaches around and finds another hand, this one hard and skeletal. As she plunges her hand through the dirt, she feels a third hand. It's moving. Massive fleshy hands bat at her, trying to save her. Or maybe himself.

Jonathan, she thinks, holding her breath. *That's who Melissa wants. She doesn't want me!*

Melissa seems to have let her go, at least temporarily, but Kayla doesn't know which way is up. She can only scramble and pray she heads toward fresh air and life, rather than scratching herself deeper into the grave.

I wrote Second Hand Dress, Haunted in late 2024/early 2025, while sorting through my wardrobe and passing along pieces to charity shops. As I mention in the Preface, I was also navigating perimenopause — a time when one's relationship with one's own body becomes strange and unfamiliar. Then I began noticing 90s retro styles everywhere, and they made me smile. So naturally, I wrote a ghost story.

Olivia's Mirror

Olivia's gaze lingers on the blue Craftsman with gray trim on the small city lot. It looks like many other houses in the neighborhood, but the presence of a long staircase and imposing retaining wall makes her feel as if she is watched from above. Yet when she looks up, no one is there.

She ascends the steps. If the table looks as good as the photo, it will be a Godsend. As a graduate student who has just been dumped and forced to pay a security deposit plus first and last month's rent, she can't really afford furniture. She rings the doorbell. A man with a thick, unruly mane of silver hair and skin marred with broken vessels answers. Opening the door wider, he says, "You must be Olivia, come in. I'm Robert."

Olivia slips inside and smells a whiff of must. Robert leads her through the parlor of mid-century furniture. Wood carved into clean lines enhances the pieces' beauty, but the upholstery is a threadbare navy blue. As she steps deeper into the home, the cold atmosphere makes her feel uneasy. Again, she feels watched. The walls, the furniture itself, understand secrets she isn't meant to learn. To calm herself, she silently questions if Robert had purchased his furniture new.

"So you're a student?" he asks.

"Yes, I'm getting my master's in history," she says.

"No wonder you enjoy antiques."

The table is as lovely as the photo: a 1960s design, with graceful, smooth lines. An out-of-place antique mirror hangs over it. It is Victorian in style, perhaps older. "All the hardware works," Robert says. "The leaf is in the table; you need to take care when it is opened and closed. Here, I'll show you."

"You said you can load it for me?" Olivia asks.

"Yes, but I want to show you the defect..."

"It's nicer than anything I have. Any defect doesn't matter."

Robert frowns. Feeling exposed, Olivia fights the sudden urge to run.

"Really, I'd rather show you the leaf mechanism, because it was tricky even when new. The last thing I need is for you to want to return it and waste my time." His cold voice suddenly softens again. "Sorry, it's just I'm trying to downsize... It hasn't been easy."

Robert goes around to the side of the table, which is pressed against the wall, shifts in enough to get around it, and points at the leaf latch below. "So this is the lock…"

Olivia follows him and bends down to examine it. Once crouched beside him, Robert lunges for her. She quickly rolls out of reach but smacks her shoulder into a cabinet. He grabs her by the shirt, then torso, and hauls her off her feet.

A ghostly form appears in the mirror: a man in an older suit with a cravat around his neck. His double chin and receded hairline give him a vague resemblance to a younger Benjamin Franklin. His mouth grows wide. He has most of his brownish teeth, but the gaps are strangely terrifying.

Olivia throws her weight to one side. Robert momentarily lets her go. She falls to the floor and scrambles to her feet, sliding on the polished wood floor. Icy tremors snake around her body as a ghostly mist encircles her. She thinks her heart stops from the cold. Her quivering lungs burn as she breathes. Her toes and fingers numb. She blinks as tears turn to ice crystals.

"My name is Samuel Peabody Wainwright," the ghost in the mirror says. "The pleasure is mine. Now, my dear young lady, I realize times have changed, but I disapprove of a lady who smokes. Tobacco and cannabis smell; the smoke damage of the Victorian age still makes my frame reek. I'm an antique, you know."

"I-I don't smoke," Olivia stammers. Her body trembles and her heart pounds with fear, but also curiosity. Sweat pools on her back and dampens her shirt, and the foul stench of a strong body odor fills her nose. She is not sure it comes from her.

Robert's posture has gone rigid, his face pallid. Ghostly ectoplasm has also encircled him. "What are you doing?" he shouts. "I've taken care of you! Fed you!"

Samuel smiles, showing the gaps in his teeth again. "I confess I should think this...uh...residential neighborhood changes much less than the life of an educated lady student. Now be quiet, while I make my decision."

Samuel turns to Olivia. "Take me with you, and I'll eat him. If not, I'll eat you. However, do not suppose you can swear to a ghost and break the pact. I am a gentleman, and my word is my bond. I will accept your word as your bond."

"You don't know what you are doing. You have to feed it every year," Robert cries, his voice raspy and raw. Robert whimpers and moans, but by how he grasps at his throat, he cannot shout again.

Olivia can't move. She hates the feeling of being frozen in place, but her terrified muscles will not budge.

"'Tis true. You must feed me a human soul each year, or I will take yours. Swear it by whatever God you believe in, or as an educated lady if you believe in none!" Samuel says.

Olivia's voice cracks, but she whispers, "I don't know what I believe. I thought you were a mirror."

"I am a ghost in a mirror..."

Robert's face turns ashen; his frown lines deepen as he struggles. "Don't I mean anything?" He punches at the glass. Olivia tries to shield her eyes, but the mirror remains intact.

Samuel shakes his finger at Robert. "You know better than that. Mere human hands cannot break my mirror. Not even a witch's curse can free me." Samuel titters as he turns back to Olivia. "And, my dear child, you must tell me your stories, and I will tell you all my stories."

"Stories?"

"Whatever 'tis you see when out with friends and neighbors. I mostly feed on gossip; I only require human souls once a year. Also my frame must be dusted, the wood oiled, and the glass shined each week. No gentleman would allow himself to fall into disarray."

"I promise!" Olivia collapses onto the floor, free from the ectoplasm that held her. She rises to her knees and gapes.

Silver light surrounds her. The air crackles with energy. Robert opens his mouth wide as if he wants to scream, but only a spittle-filled whimper leaves his mouth. He thrashes and kicks at the wall, damaging the old plaster until he tires.

Olivia's muscles tense to run; however, she remains frozen in place as she stares at the horrible scene in front of her. Samuel's and Robert's faces draw closer as tentacles of ectoplasm pull him toward the mirror. Their faces sit side by side momentarily. Robert flails his arms, trying to pull down the mirror as their faces merge. Robert's feet shudder; he stops moving. His corpse is pulled through the glass, which seems for a moment to be made of silver liquid, then solidifies.

Snapping out of her terror, Olivia backs away. A tentacle of ectoplasm reaches out and holds her fast, stronger than she possibly imagined a ghost's grip might be.

"You promised," Samuel says firmly. "I give you my word as a gentleman that you are safe with me. However, I must know: who shall you feed me?"

"But you just ate!"

Samuel smiles again, showing Olivia too many teeth. More than human. "But YOU didn't feed me."

Olivia nods slowly. "But... I have a year to figure out what to do!"

Samuel's voice grows deeper. "You promised to feed me. I supplied that food. I don't want to eat you. We need each other. I shall help you. I gave my word as a gentleman. You are quite safe with me." Though his voice is firm, his visage is soft, avuncular. "So, my dear friend, do you enjoy hosting dinner parties? I do love a good dinner party."

The realization of her situation — being trapped in a pact with an evil entity — strikes her rapidly beating heart. She knows there is only one thing to do. Her eyes blur with tears as she considers it.

"Now, my dear child, you're quite safe. There is a time for everything. If not dinner parties, I do have other...how shall I say...observant inclinations."

The very idea is shocking, but also not unwelcome. She doesn't mind being watched. This creature, Samuel, is evil, but then so is her ex. "Perhaps I could bring dates home. You could let me know what you think?" Olivia suggests, slightly more confident.

"Indeed, I shall guide you in affairs of the heart and even business. I swear I shall not hurt you, but I must feed," Samuel says.

"I can think of the first person I'll feed you," Olivia pulls out her phone to dial her ex.

Olivia's Mirror was inspired by a house on a hill that sits above one of the dance halls I frequent and the Buy Nothing Groups were I lurk.

Monday Night Hunger

The world shrank to movement and music, as always when I danced on Monday night. Indeed, the dance hall was so peculiar in its normalness that I do not know exactly why or how my mind raced or exactly what happened. Perhaps I had not drunk enough blood that day, and my throat was a bit parched. Had not my dearest friend Lilia reminded me?

Perhaps I also ought to have expected the clinging weight of exhaustion, layered with a thick sadness over the closing of the old dance hall. Maybe that was why shame found me so quickly, slipping into my mind like an old specter. Haunting me as if I were still an adolescent girl who laughed at the possible consequences of any mistakes with the gusto only the young still have. But I am no longer young, and everything I do has consequences for eternity. That is the first rule of becoming a creature of the night. Time had wormed its way into my life as it does for all things, even vampires.

I danced with a human who wanted to push my limits and his own. I told him we could take it as wild as he dared. I moved with him, matching his pace and rhythm. My body wasn't expecting his intensity, especially with hours to go. Dancing with a lead who is that powerful feels like one is being caught in a current—I needed to let ride it or become overwhelmed as his energy washed over me. I was drowning in it as I fed from his energy. Still wanting, aching for more, the song ended.

Lilia said I'd left him breathless and flustered, but I still wanted more. I always wanted more.

I should have felt triumphant. Instead, guilt slithered into my stomach, curling up tight. He was older than me, after all. His face was lined with his years, and the energy I harvested from him would most likely age him for a year or two. Then I saw others watching from the sidelines. The pressure of their eyes lanced a spike of dread through me. They weren't judging me—my brain knew they weren't—but my heart still said they were judging me for taking a public risk. I might have given him a heart attack. Even if the energy made us need less blood—there were still dangers to the dancers—especially the older ones.

Then, I felt the overwhelming presence of someone who wasn't even there. I could feel the old voice in my head, his disapproval tightening around my ribs. I imagined he would hear about this and shake his head at me. I felt sick with shame.

Ignoring this sinking utterly, I found a new partner. This man was younger and less tame, and I liked that about him. We moved together in unison. I liked the way his muscles felt under my hand, the way I fit tucked under his arm as I drew in his energy...

Suddenly, my body was drowning in terror. My stomach clenched. My pulse slammed against my ribs. Every nerve screamed—Run.

The floor tilted beneath me. No, not the floor—my body is too light and unsteady. Heat coiled in my throat, a sourness creeping up the back of my tongue. Move. Now. I staggered backward, then turned sharply, breath hitching. My vision narrowed, I was at the wall. I needed to turn. I was trapped. I heard laughter. The lights were too bright.

The faces around me blurred into hollow shapes. My feet found the ground. A hand. Reaching. His hand? No. Someone else. My dance partner. The music was still playing.

My mind caught up, dragging me back to the present. My partner froze, concern flashing across his face. He reached out gently and carefully. He asked if I was okay. I think I might have said yes, though I wasn't. But my partner had done nothing wrong, and I didn't want to think he had. It was not my dance partner, which I was afraid of.

It was the past, slipping through the cracks, seizing me by the throat. Before anyone makes assumptions, it is not my husband I feared. He would only grin and say, "Hell yeah, that's my wife!" No, it was him—the old lover who left scars no one can see.

I danced again after that. And again after that. I laughed, I smiled, I pretended nothing had happened. But I felt raw. Exposed. I had spilled something private all over the floor, a secret that should have stayed buried.

And yet. I felt something else rise up. Something sharper. Hungrier. The past thought it could haunt me forever, that he could haunt me in eternity. How easy it is to fall back into fear that I had thought was long forgotten. How easy it was to think that my bloodlust and vampiric strength kept it at bay.

But I am not the same girl he once hurt. The years had hardened me in ways I hadn't expected. I am stronger now, faster, and a vampire. And I needed to kill him before time or accident did. Yes, I must find him, take him home, and devour him whole. I will start with the fingers which once left bruises, that once cracked my head into a wall, and pressed his tongue into my mouth. Perhaps I will lean down and kiss him hard, and when his mouth opens to accept my kiss....

The cartwheels bumped, and a box of random items rattled as I rolled them over the cracked sidewalks. The streetlights flickered above me like stars. I had sought him out and found that old lover who haunted me decades later. He was older than I remembered; he might have a few more lines. But his deep blue eyes, those eyes which I had thought would be soft but were cold and calculating, were the same. Violence dripped from him like sweat from a fevered brow.

I should have done this years ago.

I didn't speak at first. Instead, I stepped closer, each movement deliberate. The ground beneath my feet felt too slippery. I stepped into the circle of his personal space, standing too close for politeness. Our size difference was too in his favor for him to be at unease. He scanned me, folding his arms across his chest. "Do I know you?"

The earth had promised that he would know my fear before his death, but I had to be cautious, yet. "I'll make sure you never forget me," I said, an ache deep in my chest. His grin was smug. My stomach churned with disgust. The same arrogance I remembered—the same sense of ownership over the world and everyone in it. With one fluid motion, I grabbed him by the collar and pulled him close, forcing him to look me in the eyes.

At first, he didn't react—not with fear, not with anger, just mild irritation, a flicker of disbelief. He smirked as if to say, What do you think you're doing? "Cute," he muttered. "I like a little roughness, but let's be adults about this." he laughed.

He didn't get it yet. He didn't see me. He certainly didn't remember me the way I remembered him. I squeezed tighter, pulling him so close that my breath ghosted across his skin. His smirk faltered. His body tensed.

"I'm going to eat you alive," I whispered into his ear.

His expression shifted, a flicker of confusion before he recovered his composure and gave me a lecherous smile. I showed him my fangs.

The pressure in the air shifted and thickened.

His bravado cracked, just a little. I enjoyed the moment — his eyes widening, his weight shifting back. His hands pushed me away from him, but I didn't budge. Then he struggled.

A tightness grew in my throat as suffocating heat emerged under my skin. I trembled, but not from fear. From something else. Something darker, more primal. I pressed my lips to his ear.

I smiled then. The kind of smile that made the air grow colder. My pulse thundered in my ears, drowning out the sound of his shallow breath as he struggled to break free. Before he could react, I leaned in close, just enough for him to feel my breath. The scent of sweat, his old leather jacket, and my deepest regrets were thick in the air. With that, I let go of him and took a step back, savoring the shock that rippled across his face. His hands twitched as if he might reach for me, but I held up a hand, a single gesture that stopped him. "You're not going to touch me or anyone else," I said, my voice icy. "Not ever again. But you will live for some of it."

The world was still silent, but the quiet between us was deafening. He stood there, frozen, as I turned to my cart. With a gentle hand on his back, I led him to sit upon it. I pushed him down onto his side and folded his legs tightly to his chest. I did not need to bind him as my power did that for me. I covered him with an old woolen blanket. Then, I set the box of random items on top and pushed him down the street. It wasn't the best of disguises, but it would do. I still have not decided how I will have my vengeance.

Only that my husband, friends, and I will consume him morsel by morsel, and he will be alive for at least part of it – but once he is gone, then I promised myself, I shall never remember him again.

And I won't. Will I?

Monday Night Hunger was originally published in Scary Stories Whispered in the Rain podcast in April 2025. It was inspired by my love of vampires and one of the panic attacks I experienced before beginning treatment for perimenopause.

Ghosts of the Internet

Sara quickly rechecks her gear as she steps lightly into the ancient pine forest. "Don't expect anything," she whispers to herself nervously. "Just enjoy the experience." She has heard this trail leads to somewhere quite special. If she goes to a certain place at a certain time, a lonely ghost of a woman named Rowena Kent who has died along the river is supposed to materialize. It is said that for the lonely she will do more than materialize. Sara doubts the veracity of the latter claim.

The trail is marked, but the cairns are easy to miss under the thick canopy of dew-covered emerald moss which drapes over the trees. The lambent golden light conceals the trail in patches of lovely green darkness. In such a place, it is easy to lose her footing or sense of direction. She glances at her compass and map and finds her place easily enough. The trail shifts north and follows a narrow and twisting path before it turns to the river. Little birds dart in and out of the cover of moss and ferns. Insects buzz about, and under ferns and between branches, spiders have made their diaphanous webs. Sara feels life all around her. Life that does not care about her at all. She is a stranger in this place. She likes that about it, though it unsettles her too. She retakes her bearings before she walks towards the misty waterfall. Underneath the trees and between the stones, Sara sees the first flowers of spring: purple and silver crocus stretching out of the cold mud. With every step closer to the river bank, she thinks about the internet myths and legends of this river. She wonders if it can be true. Can there be a specter in this wood?

A melodious voice whispers from the falls: "Come in." Yet the whisper echoes. It doesn't seem loud enough. It seems like it should be covered by the sounds of rushing water. "Come in." A hazy shape of a woman, pallid and wet, comes out of the mists of the waterfall. Her skin is too pale for health. Her hair is wet. Her fingers are blued, yet there is loveliness in the specter.

For a moment, Sara wonders if this vision is real. She cannot deny what she sees before her. She knows she should be afraid, but her heart is too lonely to be afraid. "Rowena? Rowena Kent?"

The ghost turns to face her. "Have you come for me?"

For a moment, Sara does not know what to say. She remembers the internet story. "I have heard you like pleasure."

"Pleasure is where you find it," Rowena replies. "But there is danger among the pleasure and we must be careful." She opens her gossamer gown and it drifts softly to the ground where it disappears.

"Yes, we will be," Sara says, not believing that she will be careful. She is about to make love to a ghost in the cool disquiet of the river bank.

That is when she notices the lack of birds. It is silent all around them.

"Would you like me to kiss you?" Sara asks as she unbuttons her blouse.

Rowena rises to her toes and kisses Sara's right collar bone and then her left. Next, she kneels and kisses her right nipple and then her left, before pushing the garment away.

Standing this close, Sara can hear the beat of Rowena's ferocious heart. In fact, she seems to glow. Her pallor moves from ashen to simply wan.

"Yes. I've been so lonely out here."

"I've been lonely too," Sara whispers. Sara caresses Rowena's shoulders, drawing her close. Feeling the warmth of the other woman's soft breasts against her own, she gently kisses her lips. In response, Rowena slides her tongue into her mouth as she unbuttons Sara's shorts and pushes them down. Then her panties.

"I have another idea — if you're ready for some magic?"

Sara trembles in equal measures of nerves and excitement. "I'm ready."

An iridescent, shimmering film wafts towards the women and coalesces into something more solid than a mist. Rowena presses her shoulders until Sara sits on the icy solid mist — for lack of a better word. The mist twists around her thighs. It gently teases her. As it gets higher, it begins to vibrate. Sara's pussy gets slick with excitement. Rowena's uncanny face flushes as she cups Sara's face and kisses her again. Sara feels the pressure of the mist as it shapes itself around her clit, her labia. Rowena's kissing slows as she pants and moans in pleasure. The vibrating deepens. Rowena's complexion grows brighter. A slight blush appears. She puts both hands around the back of Sara's head and tangles her hair with her fingers and gently pulls.

"Do you like that?" she asks.

"Yes. It feels so good!" Sara says. "I love it!"

Sara strokes her hands up the soft skin of Rowena's back and presses the back of her head towards her. They kiss again. Sara lightly runs the tip of her tongue over Rowena's lower lip, then gently pushes her tongue between her lips. Rowena flicks Sara's tongue with her own. The mist's quivering colors shift as Sara's pleasure grows. Her pussy becomes soaked from the effervescent trembling. Just as she thinks she might orgasm, the mist rocks back and forth as it wriggles. Sara glances down and sees the thick mist shaped as it applies pressure on her clit, then releases as if it were a hand. It does the same to Rowena. Rowena's cheeks grow red and her eyes dilate as she enjoys the pleasure. Sara grows excited to see a ghost become solid. To materialize fully in sexual desire, she thinks. No one will ever believe her.

Sara throws her head back and screams, "I'm so close!" This time the mist's tempo does not change. Instead, it repeats its rhythmic movements, pressing and releasing, until Sara comes. Moments later, Rowena yelps in pleasure.

Sara and Rowena lie back on the bed of moss, red-faced and sweaty, as the mist disappears. Sara thinks the blush spreading across the spirit's cheeks and breasts makes her even more beautiful. Sara pushes a lock of golden-red hair from the other woman's face. Rowena smiles and accepts a chaste kiss on the side of her lip.

"That was amazing!" Sara pants. She brushes her fingers through the tiny feathery fronds in the large emerald carpet. Enveloped by cold, she has to fight the after-sex sleepiness.

"Don't fall asleep," Rowena warns. "It's too cold."

When the women leave the moss-filled log, a chilly breeze

prickles Sara's skin, making her miss the caressing moss. Yet Sara admires how Rowena's round breasts and buttocks glimmer and glisten with gold spores, as does the thatch of auburn hair between her strong legs. Though Sara has enjoyed the sensual play, the vibrating mists and enchanted moss have caused a deep primal need inside her. She needs something without magic, only the satisfying touch of flesh. Rowena moves with languid contentment; Sara hopes she is interested in more lovemaking.

Light and shadow dapple the grove at an angle. The day is growing short. If Sara does not leave soon, she will have to stay the night, and of course, Rowena has not invited her to stay. Perhaps, if she is able, Rowena will escort her out of the forest if it gets too dark to find her way alone.

"I better get moving," Sara says. "It'll be dark soon."

"You won't be leaving," Rowena says.

"Of course…" Sara reaches for her discarded shorts, but her hands slip through the thick fabric. She glances at Rowena's face and recognizes her competing emotions: happiness and sadness. Relief. The blank relief of someone who has passed on a burden. Her body is with Rowena. Sara finds it hard to care at this moment as she has become another cold thing haunting the river. At least for now. She might care in the morning, or the next, but now? Right now she is with Rowena.

The women walk along the path under the thick canopy of

golden and green moss and through the dense trees. The cool breeze contrasts the cozy contentment in Sara's heart as they hike back to the trailhead. Songbirds herald their approach. Insects buzz but do not land upon either woman. With darkness falling quickly, Sara's lips brush against Rowena's and linger there. Rowena steps back first.

The spirit disappears into the darkness of her forest. Sara's spirit is alone. Not only has Rowena taken her life, but all of her hot desire, her curiosity, the pleasure of being a stranger in a living forest. In the dark. Here she lingers alone. The apparition waits for someone else to read about a ghost on the internet.

Ghost on the Internet was inspired by the myths and conspiracy theories that circulate online and weave themselves into people's lives until belief feels indistinguishable from truth.

THE LAST GASP OF ROSETON

Michelle Taylor's silver hair loosens from its ponytail ever-present wind, which never stops moving off the Pacific. Her face is lined with laughter, agony of loss. Her pants are stained, and her knees are worn, but no one is around to complain anymore about her looks. All that matters is her posture is upright. Her muscles are strong as she traverses a cracked-paved sidewalk, pulling a garden wagon which holds a bucket, clam harvester, and garbage bag. She figures she will die alone. The does not frighten her, though the possibilities of how she might die and the pain of it do. "If the road washes out..." Her mind whispers, but she smiles at her sweet memory of her husband, Dave, as they purchased their first and only house.

She murmurs sweet words to her husband's soul as she moves towards the ocean. She passes empty wood-clad houses stripped of paint. Moss, mold, and animals have taken residence in some—and of course the roses. Long ago, the town founders invested in roses to make Roseton the prettiest place by the sea. A committee planted roses in front of the shops and homes. Though many of the fragile plants died in the bitter sea air, other heartier species flourished. When the humans abandoned the town, the heartiest roses took over. Indeed, her house is the only structure on the Spit not taken by nature after her neighbors moved inland. The grocery store where she used to work is empty. The wells are poisoned by the sea, Michelle sees no reason to leave. Roseton is where her memories reside, where she can talk to Dave every day, and she can boil water.

"Undoubtedly, some houses will fall to winter, Sweetie," she whispers.

"The ever-rising tides will swallow the ones closest to the sea," the memory of her husband replies in his logical way. "Have you filled the sandbags?"

Michelle had. "I must repaint the house before winter rots the siding, but no painters will venture out to the Spit! They fear they'll get trapped by the tides as if there isn't a tide table printed every month..."

She climbs a hill covered in seagrass and gazes over to the Pacific. She remembers the electricity she felt when holding Dave's hand for the first time on this very bluff. She touches his hand with hers . She squeezes it. She touches her inner wrist remembering the way he touched her. Her inner elbow.

The soft flesh behind her ear. Only the wind can caress her now.

Or herself.

"My spirit's here with you," she tells him. The act of speaking to her late husband comforts her. "Besides where would I go?"

Dave has no reply. He doesn't know either. Their house in Roseton was bought and paid for decades ago but can't be sold. They never had much use for earthly assets, though such things would help the widow. She wasn't broke, but she didn't know how she could move either.

She is alone. There is nothing stopping her from making love to her husband on the bluff. Except that she can only make love to him in spirit and the wind is blowing off the water. No, that is better in her own home. In her own room, where the air is softer. Perhaps she will put rose petals in a bath. There certainly are enough roses to harvest. In her home with their memories surrounding her, she will make love to her husband's spirit. Her body is alive and it remembers every sweet touch.

Michelle carefully scrambles down the bluff to the muddy beach. She collects the debris that washed up on the beach overnight. Most of it is garbage, old nets, and torn fishing wires. Newly dead birds had been caught in the storm and could not escape. She sees the bloated corpse of a seal with nibbles of flesh missing. She tells Dave: "The skin might be of use."

She leaves the corpse to the animals, who will harvest it well enough. If God meant her to keep the skin, she would claim it after the next tide.

Her conversations with her late husband are abruptly interrupted by the sudden appearance of a man walking towards her. Something about his posture or gait is off-putting. Michelle readies herself. She is too old to fear a single man, and she has a knife and a can of bear spray if she really needs it.

This man is impeccably dressed as he walks along the bloody spit. His features remind her of someone, but she just can't place him. He is too elongated or perhaps stretched. He opens his mouth as if to let out a scream. Then, the earth turns to mud under his feet and swallows him. She reaches for him, but her fingers sweep right through him. He is gone. No one is there.

The tide is out. Michelle knows she is the only one on the Spit. Or is she? She had recently phoned several laborers in a nearby town. Perhaps one of them came to see if he could help. What if someone needed shelter and came to squat in an old house? Maybe he went to the wrong house, one whose subfloor is rotted or had been taken over by the roses.

She ran the rest of the way home. She called the police

station in the next town and got no answer. She left a message. Unwilling to wait for help that may not come, she gets a flashlight, two water bottles, and some bread – just in case he hasn't eaten for days. She leaves a note on her front door just in case the police come.

Starting at her next-door neighbor's house, Michelle turned the knob on the rotting door and entered the house. She gently stepped onto the rotting carpet. She called out, "Is anyone there? Hello?"

No answer.

"I'm here to help."

Michelle finds nothing but bug-ridden clothing and musty carpets. She slips through the open door of the old donut shop, the glass long having been shattered to the hearty wild rose that had flourished and taken over the building.

"Hello?" she calls.

There is a scurry and a flutter of birds at her voice, but no answer.

"Hello?" she calls again. No answer.

Michelle moves to the next house and finds more roses and animals, but there is no sound of a living human voice. She searches every empty structure on her street and the following two streets, which make up the town. She finds no other human.

"A mirage. It had to be a mirage."

She returns home and calls the police, leaving another message about her search.

Unsure what else to do, she begins defeathering the birds she collected earlier. She jumps when her phone rings. Nervously giggling, she picks up the receiver. "Hello?"

"Mrs. Taylor, we received your messages, but no one goes to that ghost town anymore except to fish or clam in season."

"I still live here."

The conversation stalls because they wanted her to leave but would not forcibly move her. She knows what has been left unsaid.

She hangs up the phone, sits in her old chair, and considers what to do. She then pens a letter to the editor to warn people who visit Roseton for fishing not to go into the old structures. She no longer has internet, but she will deliver it in the morning; after all, she could use more supplies and she should probably get the car checked out before winter.

Michelle dresses in her best clothing but realizes everything has at least a stain or tear. She finds slightly older clothing— the type she might have worn when Dave was still alive. Oh well, no one really looks at a woman her age.

"You look wonderful." Dave would have said and so she thanks him. Dave would have smiled. She loved his sweet smile.

After dropping off her editorial while waiting for the oil change, Michelle wanders down the street, reminding herself not to talk to Dave's Ghost. He isn't here in this town. This is a town of living people.

Michelle follows the smell of fresh baked bread to a small café. She orders herself a sandwich, a hot tea, a delectable-looking pastry, and local paper. She scans the headlines for missing people, but thankfully none are reported. Flipping through the rest of the paper, she notes the classifieds. She wants to stop herself, but guiltily looks through the want ads. The grocery store in the city is hiring. I could do so again, she thinks and presses the thought away. What will happen to Dave if I leave the Spit? She murmurs aloud.

"Michelle!" a woman's voice calls.

Brad and Joyce, a couple she once knew from Roseton, approach the table smiling. Michelle raises her hand in a cautious wave. She feels strangely normal, not like a strange old hermit who talks to her dead husband.

"Michelle, have you finally left the spit?" Joyce asks.

Part of her wants to say, yes.

"I'm not sure. I thought I saw someone there. I came in for help and supplies."

Brad frowns: "Not a lost child? Or teenagers messing around?"

"No, an old man. I thought...well... it's embarrassing."

"No one goes out there anymore," Joyce says. "I don't see how you manage alone. And only God knows if the road will hold for another winter."

A voice is screaming in her mind, yet her voice says: "I am tempted to move off the Spit, but I fear I'm too old to begin again."

Joyce smiles widely. "Give us your phone number, and we'll put it in our number."

Michelle realizes she forgot her phone and blushes flustered. There was so much to remember when dealing with other living humans.

"Mind?" the lady asks.

The wife writes the phone number in her newspaper. "If you need an apartment or job reference, they can call us."

"Thank you! Knowing this makes me feel better." She shakes their hands and is momentarily surprised by the warmth of their skin on hers.

She shakes the idea away. Home is home. Home is where her memories of David are. He cannot leave the Spit, as he is buried there in the old cemetery. He visits her and talks to her. She is still beautiful in his eyes.

If she leaves the Spit, she is an old woman in old fashions, in a world with cell phones and not talking to her beloved husband's ghost.

As soon as she is safely into her car and on the long gray road onto the Spit, tears crest her eyes. "Why did you have to die first?" she screams at him, but he is not there. And annoyed with herself, she sees the apparition of the screaming man with strange proportions. He is waving his hands as if to flag her down, but as she draws closer, he sinks through the pavement.

"I must stop all this crying and find him!"

Dave would've said, "That's my girl." Even though she was no longer a girl.

On the edge of town, Michelle reorganizes her supplies. She pushes down the seat, just in case the man is injured and needs to lie down.

Then she stops at the first house she sees. A large rose bush has climbed the walls. It's thorns prick at her as she pushes open the door. She gently tests the floor at the threshold, and calls out, then listens.

The process continues until she comes to the mayor's old residence. She stops short. There is the man she has seen. James Moore, the founder of the town. The facial likeness is uncanny, but standing in front of her, his proportions are normal. He is not stretched. But of course, he has been dead for a hundred years or so.

She pushes past the masses of thorned roses bushes as she presses the rotting wood door open. "Hello?"

Sunlight spills through moth-eaten curtains. This room feels alive, though mold covers the rotting wallpaper. Insects race across the wall and disappear into unseen holes at the sound of her footsteps. Stepping into the main room, Michell feels someone or perhaps the room itself sucking energy away from her body. She shivers. What appears to be James Moore with all his strange proportions appears to sit in front of an unlit fireplace. The lanky frame rises from his seat. The air crackles as the blight approaches, following the ghost's drifting form. He towers above her but his milky eyes do not focus upon her.

"Six generations of his family and hers have lived on this spit of land. The sea will take it if you leave...You must stay here."

"Is my husband here?" Michelle asks.

James Moore shakes his head. "What is one man to the history of this town?"

Michelle's heart drops. Dave isn't here.

James Moore reaches toward her, but swirls of icy ether bite at Michelle's skin. He gives an ear-piercing scream that echoes across the room, causing more plaster dust to fall from the ceiling and insects to go scurrying.

She is trapped. The Spit, her memories are binding her.

Stumbling on the loose floorboards, Michelle backs, closer to the door. She senses the sunlight changing as the wind brings more clouds to shore.

The ghost of James Moore surges forward and grasps at her wrists. His screams echo, and birds take flight. Panic grips her. Her heart pounds in her chest, she cannot breathe. She yanks herself away and bursts through the front door, the roses grasp onto her and piercing her with their thorns.

Quickly, Michelle hurries to her car. Mist wets her windshield. Soon, the rain will come.

She speeds to her house, until her wheel hits a pothole. Remembering the state of the road, she slows.

Once home, she races to pack all her clothing and old jewelry in two suitcases. She saves her photo box of the pictures she saved from the last flood. She pulls her old wedding portrait off the wall and hurries out to the car. She shoves these items into the car's trunk.

The shape of James Moore reaches for her and tries to pull her back. He screams, "You can't leave." The mist coalesces into a steady drizzle.

Michelle races back into the house. She grabs her mother's old cookbook and an anniversary clock which she wants to keep. Then the old silver, which she will most likely pawn for scrap. Nothing else has worldly value. Most of it is garbage collected from the beach. Everything else can be replaced.

The sun has not set, but dark clouds swirl off the coastline.

James Moore tries to bar her path, she plows through him and into her car.

As she drives along the beach road, James Moore screams, he wildly waves his arms as if he can beat back the tide and incoming storm.

Waves splash across the low road, coating her windshield in brackish water. Knowing the road's state, Michelle drives cautiously, determined to leave Roseton.

The Last Gasp of Roseton was originally published in Scary Stories Whispered in the Rain podcast in January 2025. It was written during a period of grief and, as mentioned in the Preface, out of a deep fear of losing my husband who is alive and well.

No One Else To Touch

Time speeds up when you get older. I didn't know it would slur together in such an absurd way that I can't remember exactly how it happened. I only know I am confused and frustrated and truly struggling to get my words from my brain to my mouth! I can't always remember the names of the two young nurses who come by to ensure my health.

Yet some days I wonder the point of them. If I chose to, I could stop. They are here because I pay them, if I stop payment, they stop too.

The day nurse ensures my comfort. She asks if I wish to be moved. The Gloom's unending presence is why I struggle to move when there are patterns in the drywall. I have outlived everyone I have ever loved. My husband is gone, buried for nearly twenty years. I outlived my only child. My parents are gone. My sisters are gone. Their children have forgotten me. Perhaps this is my fault. Family does not mean what it once did.

Perhaps, that is for the best.

Once the day nurse leaves, I look across the expansive desert. Out my window on the hill, I see the red ridge and the dry forest beyond. Rising above the forest is a ridge, a plateau. Beyond that the unending horizon of blue and pale peach. I stare at this view until the light changes.

The night nurse arrives. She helps me undress and bathe, but her clinical touch feels worse than nothing. Once some would look at my home and material assets and the photos of friends and relations and say my life is rich. But they actually mean WAS rich. I hiked mountains, I dove into lakes. I danced without care. Those memories bring me, now stuck in a brittle body, both pleasure and pain.

The Gloom is contained sometimes. It comes out others. I hate when it comes out. These people are kind, but they are not my friends. I feel so dead, yet I linger. A cold weight sits on the edge of the bed at night. My eyes can't stay open.

I feel the presence linger beside me. My body is so tired, yet, I think if I just sit up, if I reach out, I might feel it the way I used to ache for my husband. And then I feel the cold hand through my blankets tucking me in. I imagine the way my husband used to hold me. I imagine his strong arms around me. The way I once rested my head on his shoulder. The way his hand felt in my hand. The way his hands felt on my once-supple body. Yet, the cold hands warm my withered body until blackness and dark dreams take me. Yet, the dawn comes again. I groggily rise and wander into the bathroom. Then the kitchen. I am best in the morning. Still today, I feel the decline sharply.

A shadow haunts the corner at breakfast. It could be glaucoma. Or is it Death? Has Death finally come for me?

I cannot be afraid. I am grateful. For the first time in years, something, no, some presence is paying attention to me.

I make myself scrambled eggs with cheddar cheese. I melt the cheese under the broiler. Then I move to pour myself orange juice. I set my meal on the table and, like the lady I am, I set my napkin in my lap.

The shadow morphs into something bigger. I still do not feel fear. It is something else. Excitement? Why not? This is the start of a new adventure. Perhaps my soul will just sleep into darkness and I will be worm food. While I know what I might prefer, it's hard to care which. I take a bite of my breakfast and then another. The shadow does not speak. I turn to it. "I'm tired of pretending you aren't there. I want to touch you," Death whispers. "I want to touch you, but there is no turning back once you take my hand."

I slam down my fork. My plate of eggs clatters against the table. Death takes a deep breath. I rise to my feet. I take a shaky step and reach out a hand that now trembles.

"I want to know you," I say.

Death rises, but does not step back from my grasping whithered hand. I will touch Death, because there is no one else to touch in this world.

No One Left to Touch was also written during a period of grief. It explores not only the importance of physical touch, but the human connections that give touch its meaning.

About the Author

Elizabeth Greyrose is an illustrator and author based in Seattle, WA, who believes art should be beautiful, uncompromising, and occasionally terrifying -- just like her. When not writing or illustrating, Greyrose can be found dancing the waltz or west coast swing, life drawing bees, baking treats for her friends, and lake swimming.

She shares short stories and recipes on her

Patreon: https://www.patreon.com/elizabethgreyrose

and Instagram: @elizabeth_greyrose